900 BUCKETS OF PAINT

900 BUCKETS OF PAINT

By Edna Becker · Pictures by Margaret Bradfield

New York ABINGDON PRESS *Nashville*

TO MY BROTHER'S FAMILY NEXT DOOR:

HOWARD, EVELYN, BONNIE AND JIMMY

ONCE THERE WAS an Old Woman who lived in a little red house that stood beside a laughing brook, right in the middle of a field of clover. With her lived her two cats, Pansy and Violet, and her donkey, whose name was Arthur, and her cow, Bossy.

The Old Woman's house had once been a very bright red. But the sun and wind and rain had beaten against it until it was faded and worn. One day the Old Woman decided that it looked too shabby to live in any longer. So she decided to move.

She began packing early the next morning. By noon she had all her belongings loaded into the donkey's cart. All, that is, but her alarm clock. She set this inside the cupboard with glass doors until it was time to start. Then she brought the cats down from the attic.

The Old Woman hitched the donkey to the cart and tied the cow behind. Then she climbed up onto the seat of the donkey cart. She put Pansy on one side of her and Violet on the other. And off she drove, forgetting all about her clock.

When the Old Woman reached the first corner, she turned to the right. Then she kept on going straight ahead until at last, far down the road, she spied a little yellow house all freshly painted.

"I think I'd like to live here," she said to herself as she drove into the yard.

She tied Arthur to a post and went to see if anybody lived there. Nobody did, so she set about at once unpacking her belongings. By evening she was nicely settled.

The next morning the Old Woman overslept dreadfully, not having her alarm clock. Just the same, when she woke she felt very well satisfied with herself.

"How do you like it here?" she asked Pansy and Violet.

The cats waved their long tails. *Meow*, they said. "Fine. There are plenty of mice in the attic."

After breakfast the Old Woman went out to milk the cow.

"How do you like it here, Bossy?" she asked.

Bossy rolled her big brown eyes. *Moo!* she said. "Very much indeed. The clover is sweet and tender, and there is plenty of it."

The Old Woman, feeling very happy, went to give the donkey a bucket of water.

"How do you like it here, Arthur?" she asked.

Hee, haw! brayed Arthur. "I think it is terrible!"

"Why, Arthur!" cried the Old Woman. "What is wrong?"

"I won't drink out of a bucket, so there!" said Arthur. And he stamped his foot.

"Why, what is the matter with a nice clean bucket?" asked the Old Woman.

"I want to drink out of a laughing brook," stormed Arthur. And he would not drink out of the bucket.

All the next day Arthur grumbled and complained.

At last the Old Woman packed up her belongings and set out to find a house that had a laughing brook for the donkey to drink from.

When she reached the first corner, she turned to the right. Then she kept on going straight ahead until at last, far down the road, she spied a little bright green house. A laughing brook ran close by.

"I think I'd like to live here," she said to herself. Nobody lived in the house, so the Old Woman set about at once unpacking her belongings. She found the house very comfortable.

The next morning Pansy and Violet were merrily running around in the attic, catching mice. Arthur was down at the brook, drinking. The Old Woman, feeling very happy, went to milk the cow. But Bossy would not give her any milk.

"Why, Bossy!" scolded the Old Woman. "What is the matter?"

Mmm, moaned Bossy. "I don't like it here. There isn't enough clover."

"I will get you some hay," the Old Woman promised.

"I don't want hay. I want clover," grumbled Bossy.

"What shall I do?" sighed the Old Woman. "I'll just have to move again."

The next morning the Old Woman packed up and set out to find a house that had a brook and a clover field, too. She sighed as she drove away, for she liked the little green house.

When the Old Woman reached the first corner she turned to the right. Then she kept on going straight ahead until at last, far down the road, she spied a little low-roofed house. She didn't like the house very well, but there was a laughing brook beside it and a field of clover around it. Nobody lived there, so the Old Woman set about at once unpacking her belongings.

The next morning after breakfast the Old Woman went out to milk the cow. Bossy was nibbling contentedly at the clover. Arthur was down by the brook.

The Old Woman carried back to the house the brimming bucketful of milk Bossy had given her and poured out a big saucerful for Pansy and Violet.

"Here, kitties!" she called.

But Pansy and Violet did not come. At last the Old Woman found the cats, sulking in a corner.

"For gracious' sake," she said. "What is the matter?"

Meow, meow! whined Pansy and Violet. "There isn't any attic in this house and we can't find any mice. We won't live here."

The Old Woman rushed from one room to the other, trying to find a way to the attic. But the cats were right. There wasn't any attic.

"Whatever shall I do?" she sighed.

There was nothing for her to do but to pack up and move once more.

She started out the next morning. When she reached the first corner, the Old Woman turned to the right. Then she kept on going straight ahead for a long, long way. At last, far down the road, the Old Woman spied a little white house. There was a clover field around it, and it looked high enough to have an attic.

"Now if there is only a brook," the Old Woman said to herself.

Just then the wheels of her cart rumbled over a little bridge, and there was the brook.

"This is the very place for us!" she thought as she drove into the yard.

As she was getting out of the cart, a man came around the corner of the house with a paint bucket in his hand. The Old Woman's heart sank.

"Do you live here?" she asked.

"Oh, no," replied the man cheerfully. "I've just been painting the house. You see, a man gave me nine hundred buckets of paint. I wasn't very busy, so I thought I'd paint all the houses around here that looked shabby. It will make things look much better."

"That is certainly kind of you," replied the Old Woman. "Will it be all right for me to move in here with my two cats, my donkey, and my cow?"

"Certainly, certainly," said the painter. "Move right in. I'll finish the fence, then I'll be leaving."

The Old Woman began unpacking. As she put some plates into the cupboard with glass doors, she saw something that surprised her very much. It was an alarm clock.

The Old Woman took it out and looked at it carefully.

"Well, I declare," she said at last. "I do believe this is my own clock. I remember now that I forgot it when I moved the first time. I wonder . . ."

The Old Woman went to the door.

"Oh, Mr. Painter!" she called out. "Do you happen to remember what color this house was before you painted it white?"

"It was red," the painter shouted back. "But it was very old and faded. That's why I painted it."

"Well, I declare!" said the Old Woman again. "Well, it was a nice vacation!"